MELODY
LEARNS
EVERYTHING

WRITTEN BY YORK ELVIE

ILLUSTRATED BY PAUL PODGER

THIS IS DEDICATED TO MY LITTLE GIRL

&

ALL THE CHILDREN OUT THERE
IN HOPES THEY REMEMBER THEY
CAN LEARN LOTS OF NEW THINGS.

Well what a story I have to tell you!

It's about a very smart and
adorable baby girl named Melody.
I'm not saying she is the smartest,
just **VERY VERY** smart!

Now what makes this baby Melody
SOOO smart? Well since this is
your introduction to Melody,
I will start at the beginning.

Baby Melody was small at first but decided
that her personality wasn't going to be small.
She quickly decided that she wanted to learn...

EVERYTHING!

First, she learned to crawl... but then she said,

"THIS IS TOO SLOOW!"

So she started walking... Then started
RUNNING ALL OVER THE PLACE!

In the park... in the house... and even...
up the WALLS and on the CEILING!

She would tire her parents out...

You would think that she was done learning.

BUT NO!
She was just getting started!

After she felt she had mastered walking and running, she began **CLIMBING!**

She climbed couches and mommy and daddy and walls and **HILLS and MOUNTAINS!**

Her parents were very tired...

You would think that she was
done learning now right?

BUT NOO!

She was just getting started!

Melody discovered **ART!**
She was building and painting like
no other baby in the history of babies.

(I believe her art is hanging in the
Art Gallery of Ontario.)

Melody's Parents were still very tired...

I know what you're thinking...
She has to be done learning now!

BUT NOOO!
She was just getting started!

What she did next was truly amazing...
Melody started **COOKING!**
She didn't just warm things up in the microwave...
She was cooking full meals!

Rice, chicken, vegetables,
ribs, fried dumplings!
It was amazing to watch
but even more amazing to eat!

Melody had tired parents... but they ate well!

Before you even ask... **NOOOO!**
She wasn't done learning!
SHE WAS JUST GETTING STARTED!

Melody discovered her voice next,
she began **SINGING!**

She sang nursery rhymes, songs she heard
on the radio and even her own songs!

(Melody became such a good singer,
I believe she had a concert at a BIIIG stadium.)

Melody's parents were **ALWAYS** tired.

But what Melody learned to do
the best was be a good daughter
and love her mommy and daddy even
though they were still **VERY VERY** tired!

You would think that she was done learning now...
But No. She was just getting started!